Chinese Kites

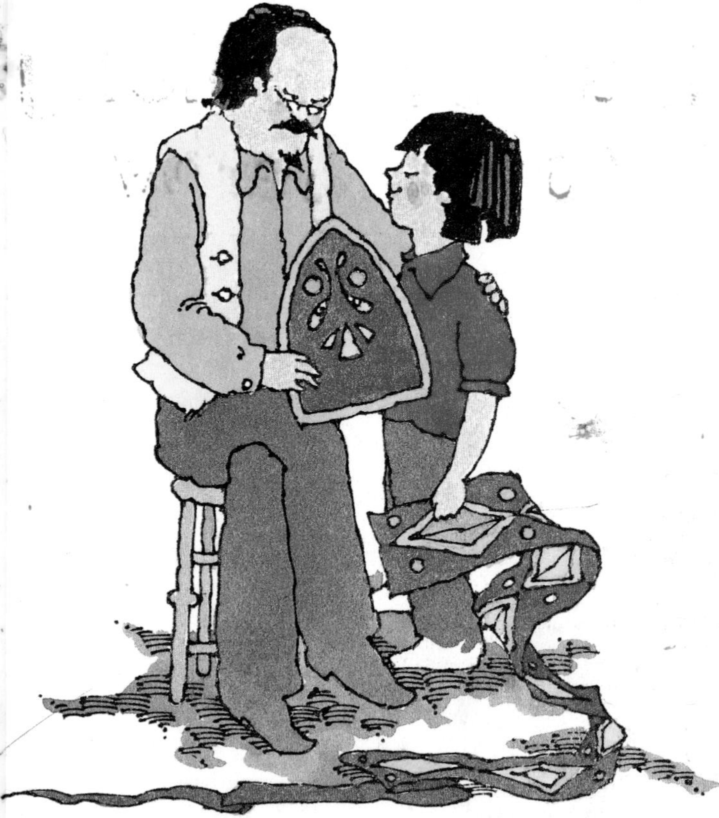

By Rebel Williams
Illustrated by Fred Harsh

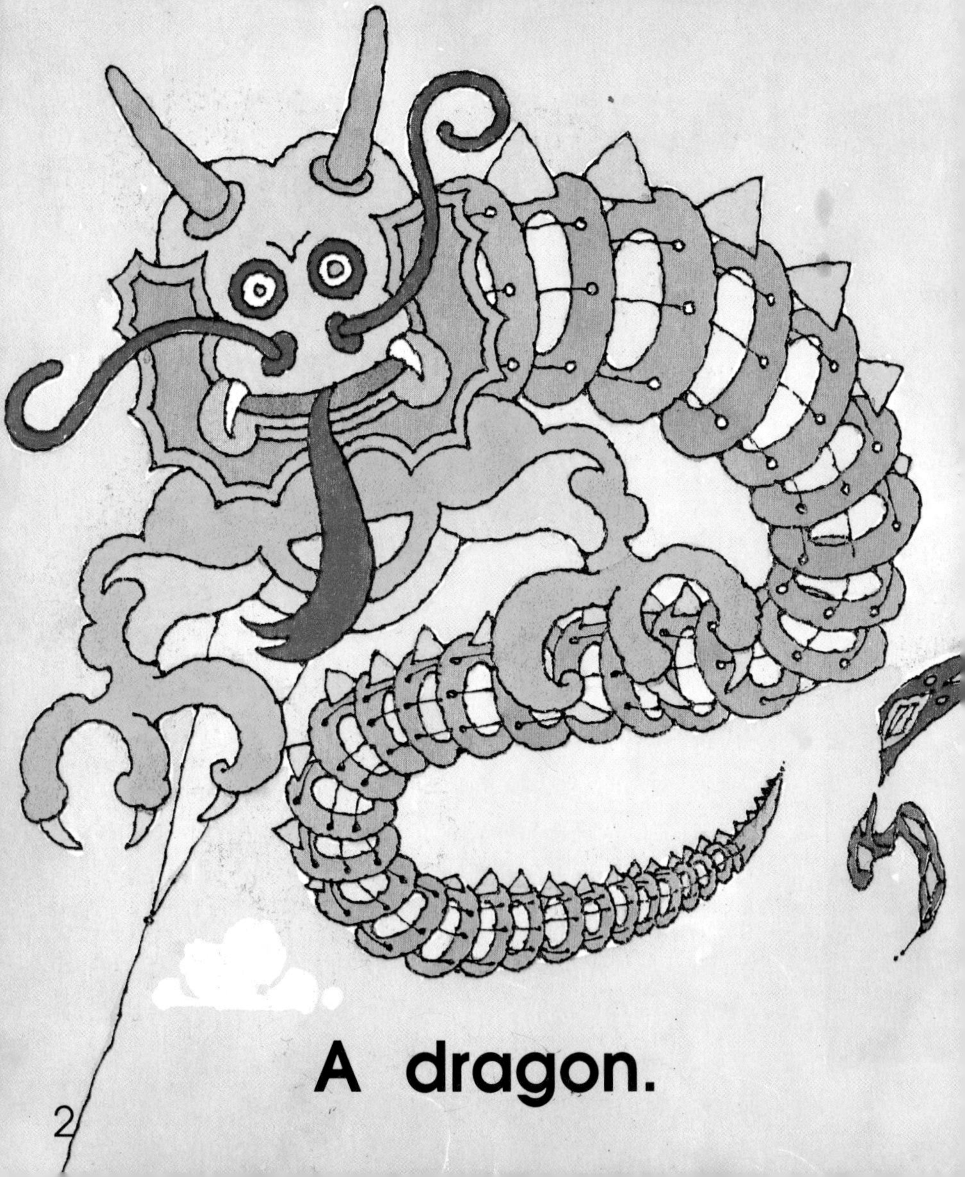

A dragon.

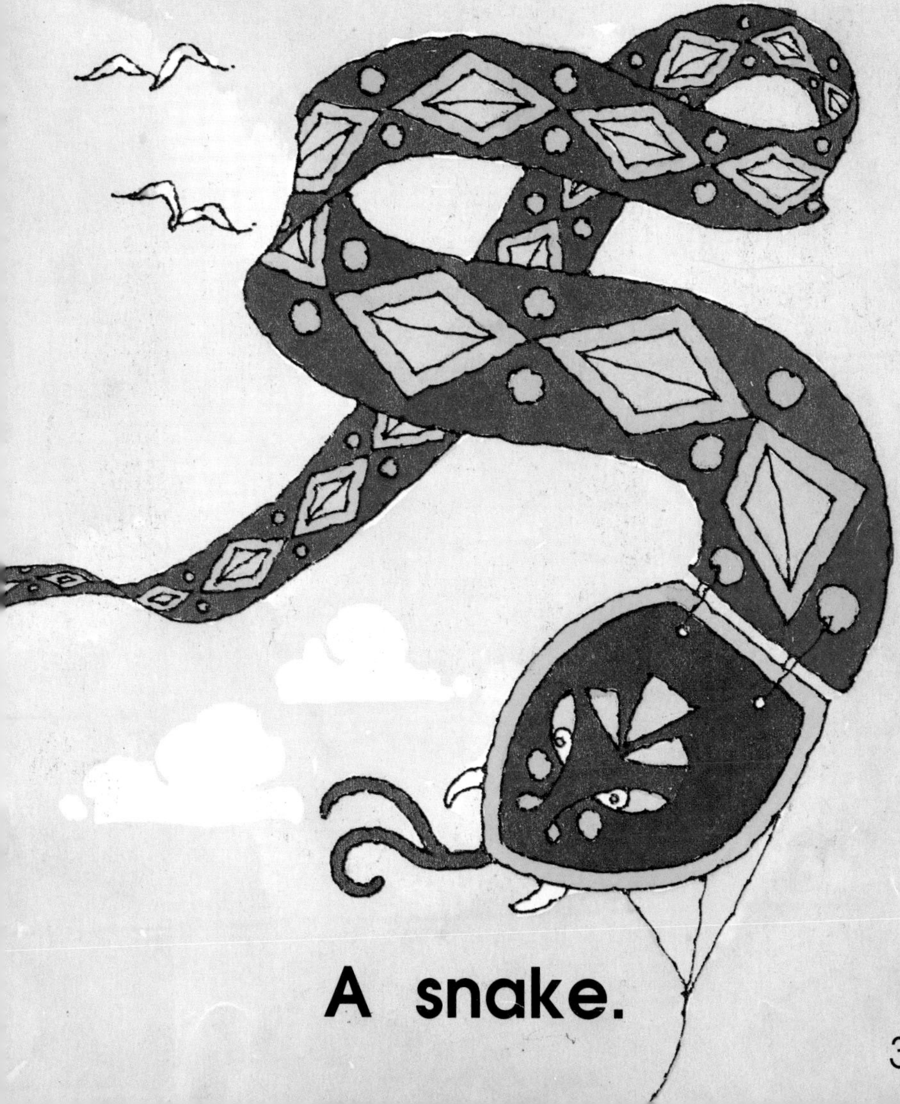

A snake.

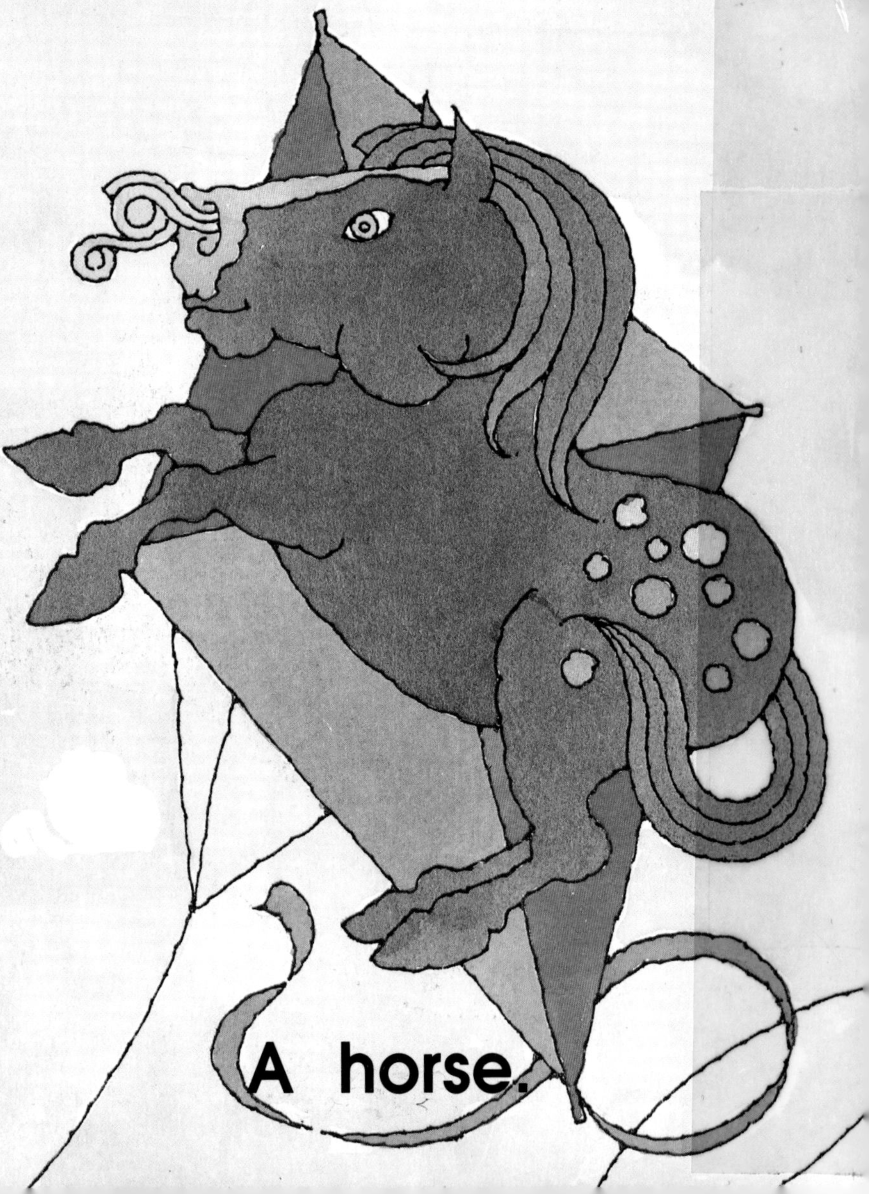

A horse.

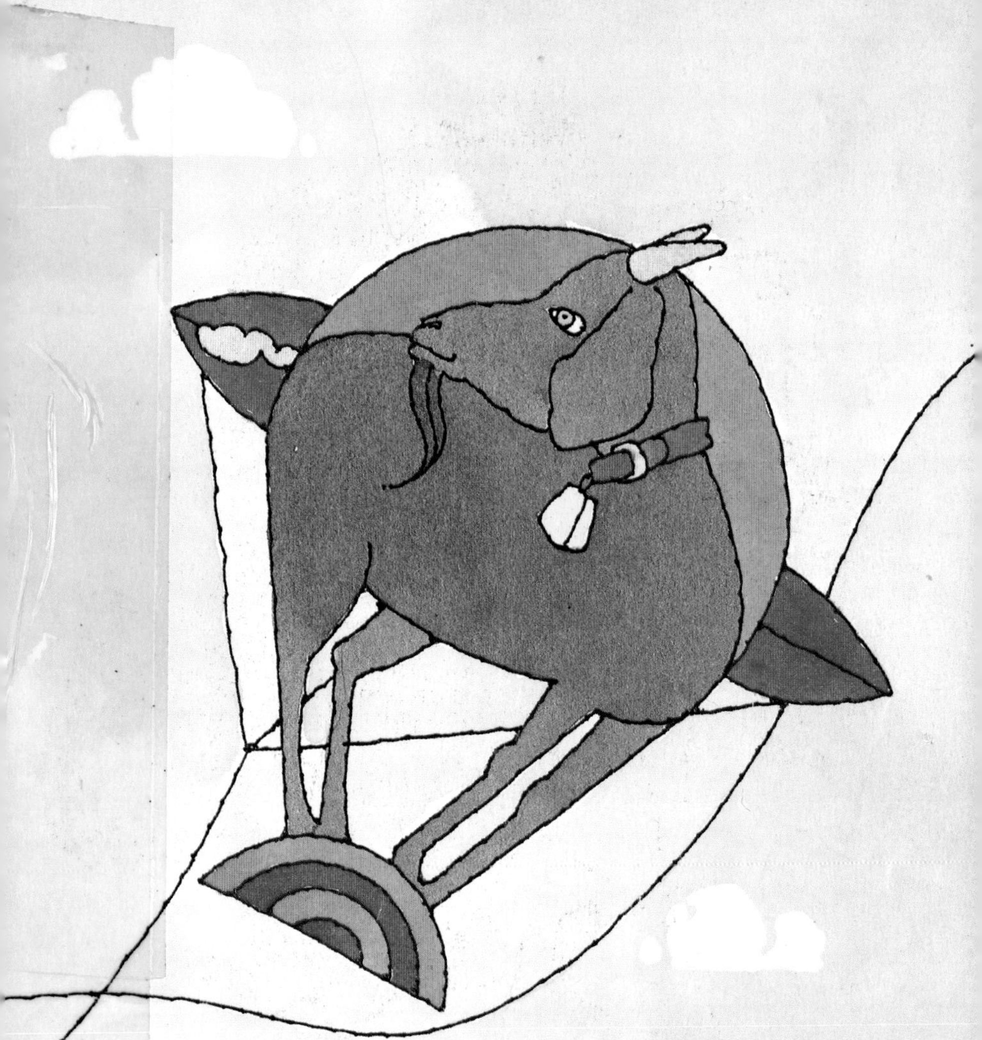

A goat.

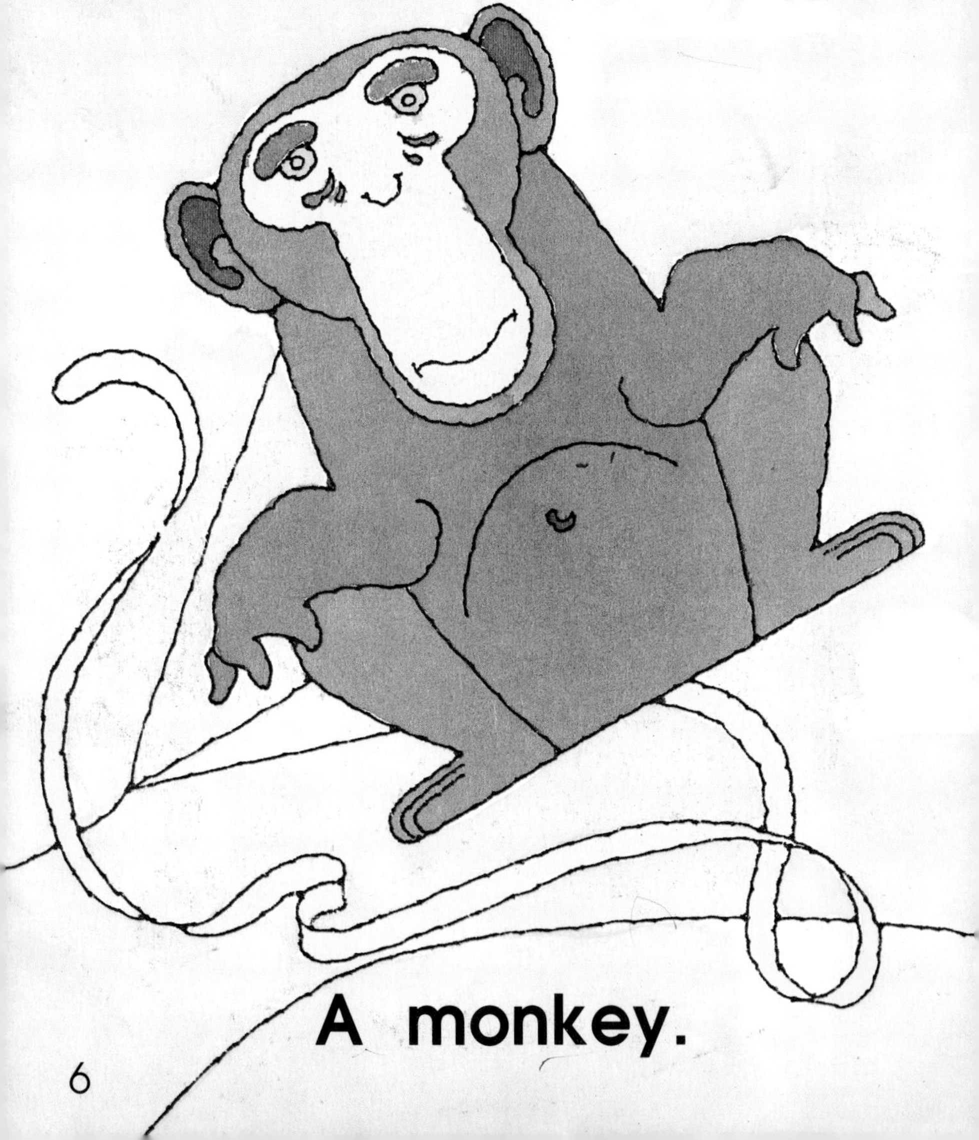

A monkey.

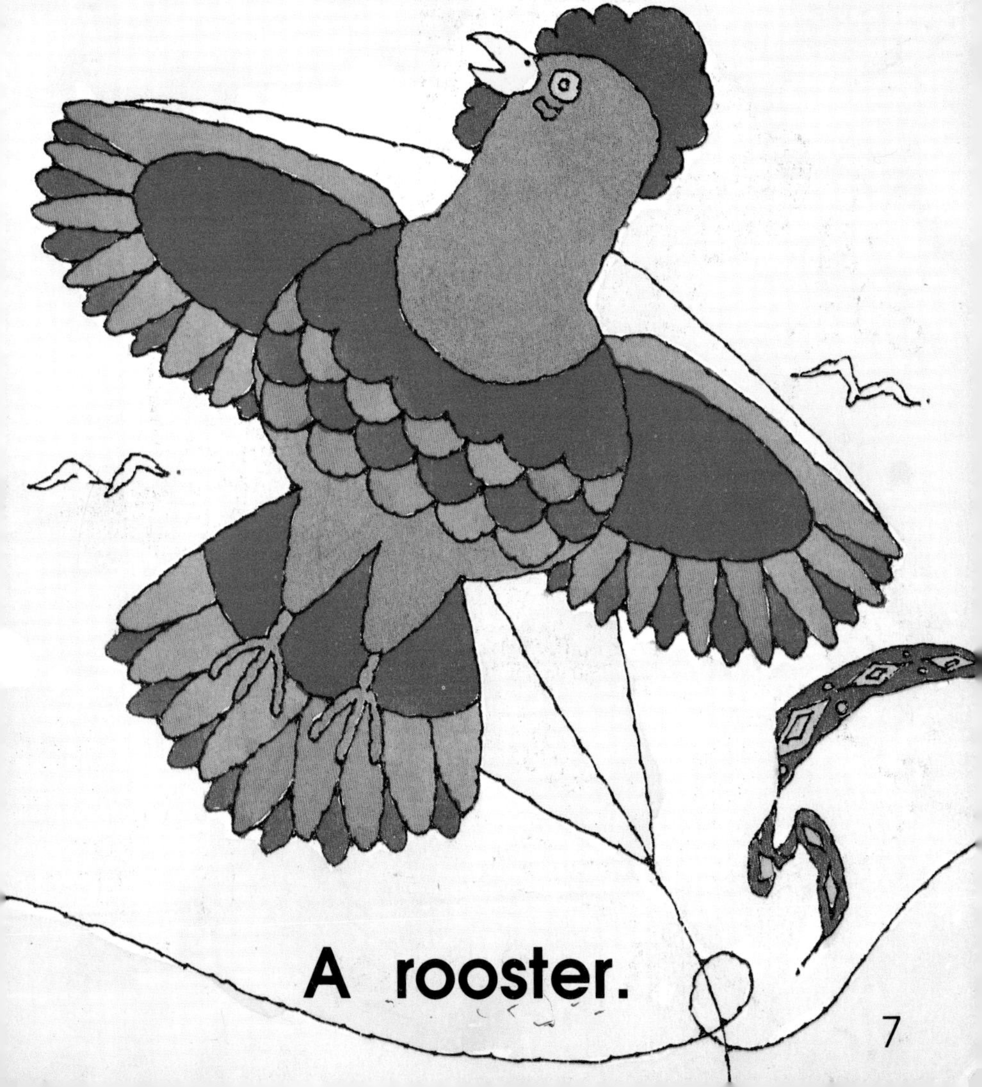

A rooster.

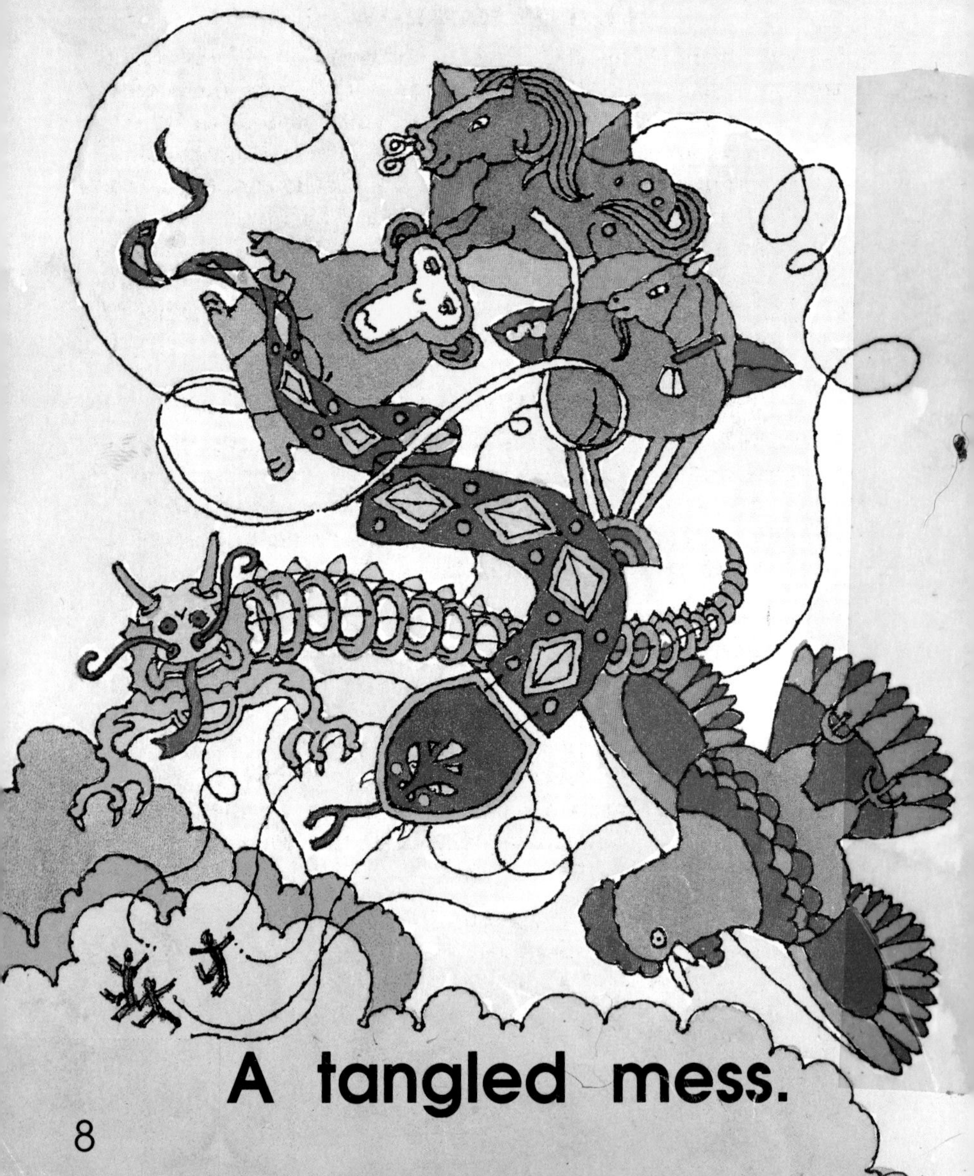

A tangled mess.